NEW CASTLE COUNTY

Happy as a Tapir

BY
Terry Carbone
ILLUSTRATED BY
Keith DuQuette

VIKING

The illustrations for *Happy as a Tapir* were completed through the combined use of colored pencil, watercolor, and gouache applied on a series of watercolor grounds.

VIKING
Published by the Penguin Group
Viking Penguin, a division of Penguin Books USA Inc.,
375 Hudson Street, New York, New York 10014, U.S.A.
Penguin Books Ltd, 27 Wrights Lane, London W8 5TZ, England
Penguin Books Australia Ltd, Ringwood, Victoria, Australia
Penguin Books Canada Ltd, 10 Alcorn Avenue, Toronto, Ontario, Canada M4V 3B2
Penguin Books (N.Z.) Ltd, 182–190 Wairau Road, Auckland 10, New Zealand

Penguin Books Ltd, Registered Offices: Hardmondsworth, Middlesex, England

First published in 1992 by Viking Penguin, a division of Penguin Books USA Inc.

1 3 5 7 9 10 8 6 4 2

Library of Congress Cataloging-in-Publication Data

Carbone, Teresa A.
Happy as a tapir / by Teresa A. Carbone : illustrated by Keith Du Quette.
p. cm.
Summary: When the zoo animals gather to trade animal suits and change identities, as they do twice a year, the tapir is told that he must remain a tapir until he gets it right.
ISBN 0-670-84227-3
[1. Tapirs – Fiction. 2. Zoo animals – Fiction.] I. Du Quette, Keith, ill. II. Title.
PZ7.C187Hap 1992 [E] – dc20 91-36480 CIP AC

Printed in Hong Kong
Set in 16 pt. Esprit Book

To Grandpa,

the tapir,

and Alison

—T.C.

To Mom, Dad,

and the animal kingdom

—K.D.

At the end of each zoo-day, when the sun has just set and the people have all gone home, the great zoo gates close behind them.

Then the animals say to each other, "A day's work well done!" They leave their cages one by one and make their way to the grove in the park near the elephant house.

As it grows dark they unbutton, unzip, and step out of their work suits of feathers and fur. They shake them and brush them and hang them on trees. And now without their trunks, tails, or spots, they gather together and sit in a ring, to talk of the zoo-day and all that is new.

But two nights a year are different from the rest. On two nights each year, in spring and in fall, they trade off their costumes for ones that are new, choosing other wonderful animal suits.

And as they sat in a ring on one pretty spring night, the oldest among them, who was kind and wise, passed on the elephant suit that he'd worn with pride. He said to his friend who'd be elephant next, "Remember that elephants are patient and strong, and clever to manage that very long trunk."

Two others were trading, a leopard and a bear. "Oh, now I'll be a leopard with all those fine spots. I'll be jazzy and graceful, and fast now, you'll see!"

Orangutan and walrus, kangaroo and giraffe, they all found new owners as the evening went on.

But just when they thought they might go off to bed, a small voice from the side said, “Well, what about me?” They all turned and looked at the one on the end who seemed quite unhappy.

“I’ve not made a trade like everyone else. I’ve been this old tapir since I came to the zoo, and now it’s my chance to become something new. There are so many things that I’d just love to be, like a lion or rhino or a tall feathered ostrich with a wonderful neck.”

“Well, no, not yet,” said the one at his side. “You see, you’re the newest one of us here. You’ll have to wait longer before you’re ready to trade. I waited myself when I came to this zoo, until I was told that I’d done my job well. So just be a tapir a bit more for now, and soon you can trade and be part of the fun!”

So they gathered their new suits as the moon rose above, and said their good nights with a smile and a nod. But the tapir stood alone, and thought, “Well, just wait. I’m as clever as they. I can be other animals, any kind, they will see! I can walk like them, talk like them, jump, climb, and swim.” So he left with a frown and the old tapir suit, off to dream of great animals, any animals, but not tapirs!

The next day he waited for people to come. "They'll get more than a tapir, they'll love what they see." He ran straight up a tree and howled like a monkey! He did balancing tricks that he'd seen the seals do. The silly young tapir got sillier still as he buried his long tapir head in the sand!

The people could hardly believe what they saw. He heard one of them say, "That's not what tapirs do!" Others just passed him by. But he thought to himself, "This was better by far than being that dusty old tapir again." He would tell all the others, and he'd tell them with pride, of all the animals he'd been in just one single day!

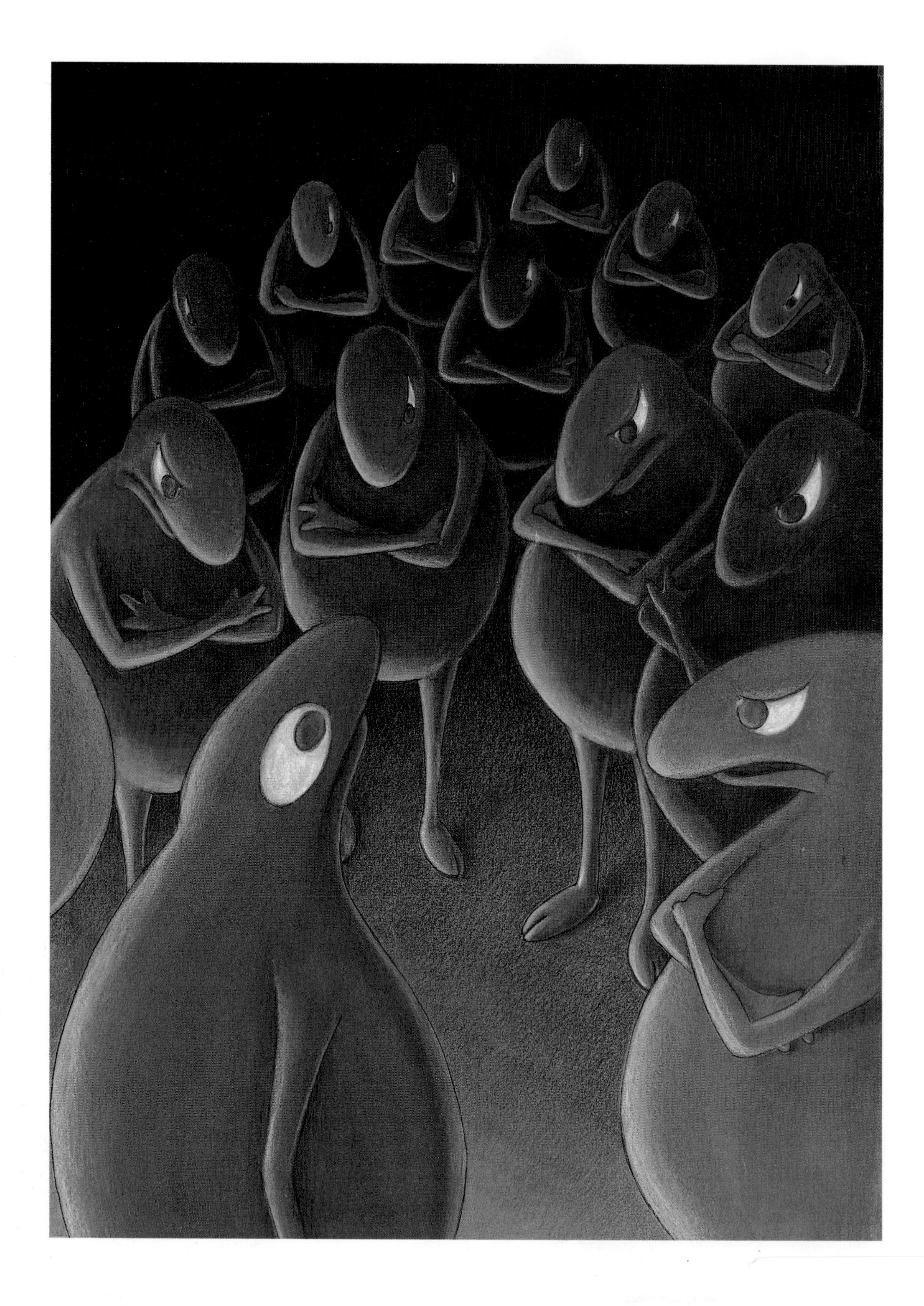

He squirmed with excitement when the evening arrived. But the others looked stern as they gathered around.

The oldest among them stood above him and boomed, “How silly you’ve been! Just what did you mean, doing so many things! While you’re a tapir, you must be just that. You must walk like one, talk like one, eat what one eats. You must wear your suit proudly for the people to see. When they come to the tapir, that’s what they want, not a monkey who howls, or a seal or a bird! You won’t be another animal till you’re a tapir just right!”

They marched off together and left him alone. Under the light of the bright round moon, he found his way back to the tapir house. He walked straight to the zoo sign and read what it said:

Tapirs belong to a family of prehistoric mammals related to horses and rhinoceroses. They have short legs and long snouts. They are shy and like to be alone but they enjoy bathing and eating buds and leaves.

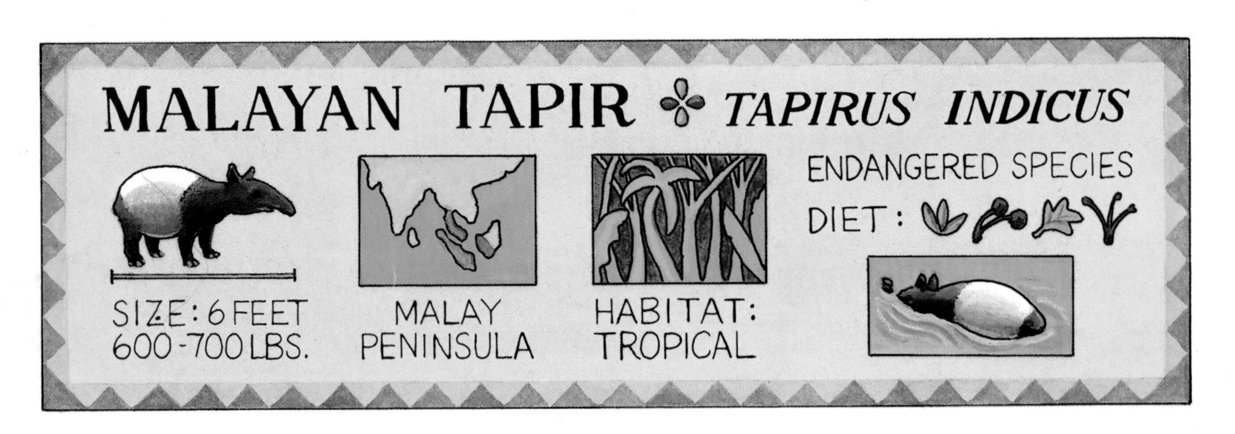

He read it again and again until he knew every word by heart. Then he went off to bed with a yawn and a smile, thinking, "Yes, if a tapir is what I must be, why, I'll be the best tapir this zoo's ever seen!"

The very next day when the people came, they found a shy tapir who peeked at them through the green leaves and happily slipped into his stream for a swim. He reached for small buds with his long sniffing snout as he thought of green jungles where shy tapirs live.

Each day more people came, and the tapir knew why. He did tapir things better–why, he did them the best. And night after night, as they sat by the fire, he told his friends tapir tales, every last thing.

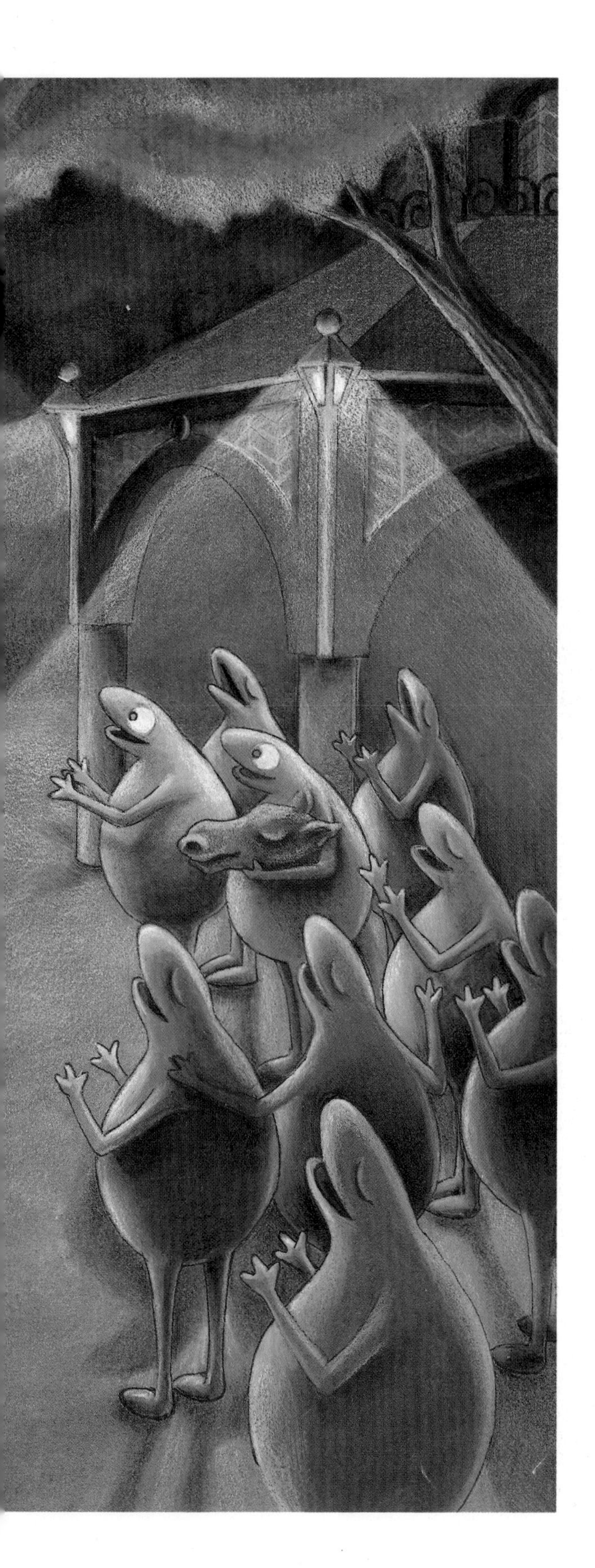

The spring and summer turned into fall, and then came the magical night, the second each year, when they traded their work suits for ones that were new.

So they gathered again, and as it grew dark, they joined hands in excitement and sang out a song. All but the tapir who just took his seat.

They all turned and looked at him, and the oldest one said, “We think you’ve done quite a fine job. You’ve been the best tapir this zoo ever had. Now what animal would you like to be next?”

"Well, you see," said the tapir, "I don't want to switch. I'm quite pleased as a tapir. It suits me just fine. I've found out that I like to be shy and to swim and eat little pink buds and green leaves –"

"Now see here," interrupted the one at his side, "I am sorry, you must change. It's how our zoo works. We shall have to insist that you turn in your suit. We're all ready and waiting. The trades must begin."

So he sighed very sadly, looking slowly around, and began to unzip and unhook and undo the same tapir suit he now loved as his own.

"Just look at your choices! You're as free as a bird! Be a bear or a zebra . . . or a camel . . . ," his friends said.

"Well, I'd like something fun,
and a little bit odd."

"Try a kangaroo then! You can stand on two legs. You can jump very high, and you'll have that fine pouch!"

"Well, all right," he decided, as they passed him the suit. "I'll try hard, that I promise. I won't let you down."

He gathered his things and said his good nights, and then went off alone to prepare for the day.

In the morning, dressed in his kangaroo suit, he
greeted his visitors with a hop and a bounce.
He jumped and he bounded all that
day and the next, and the people
laughed and clapped and
came back for more. But
each night he grew sadder.
It just wasn't for him.
"It's a tapir I want to be,"
he thought to himself,
"but how will I do it? . . .
How long can I wait?"

He waited for spring and that one special night when they gathered to trade off their suits once again. As it grew dark in the grove in the park, he put on the tapir head and stood up to speak. "I won't be taking a new suit this time. You see, I've decided I must leave the zoo. If I can't be a tapir, I don't want to stay. I've been so unhappy being something else."

"But you must stay!" "You can't go!" they joined in at once. "We would miss you." "We need you!"

"No, you'll find someone else who can take on my part. I'll be off in the morning. I'm sure this is right."

The next morning before all the people arrived, all his friends gathered round to tell him good-bye. One by one they each gave him a hug and a pat, and they wished him sunny days, nice new friends, and good luck.

"I'll miss you, too," he called back to his friends as he passed through the zoo gates for the very last time.

ZOO

ZOO

But at that same moment he felt something odd! He felt four short legs! A long snout! Could it really be true?

"He's a tapir!" his friends cried from inside the zoo.

"That I am!" he yelled back as he danced off with glee.

And a tapir he was from that very day on.

A tapir for real.

And the happiest still.